The Adventures of Dock and Nettle

By

James L P Johnson

Grosvenor House
Publishing Limited

All rights reserved
Copyright © James L P Johnson, 2021
© Illustrations by Lyn Stone

The right of James L P Johnson to be identified as the author of this
work has been asserted in accordance with Section 78
of the Copyright, Designs and Patents Act 1988

The book cover is copyright to James L P Johnson

This book is published by
Grosvenor House Publishing Ltd
Link House
140 The Broadway, Tolworth, Surrey, KT6 7HT.
www.grosvenorhousepublishing.co.uk

This book is sold subject to the conditions that it shall not, by way of
trade or otherwise, be lent, resold, hired out or otherwise circulated
without the author's or publisher's prior consent in any form of binding or
cover other than that in which it is published and
without a similar condition including this condition being imposed
on the subsequent purchaser.

This book is a work of fiction. Any resemblance to
people or events, past or present, is purely coincidental.

A CIP record for this book
is available from the British Library

ISBN 978-1-83975-373-2

For George, a child who has inspired the many qualities
contained within this book

Early Spring

Soap Boarding

Make sure to use it, and make sure to let them.

Dock and Nettle were bored, so they decided to run through all of the rooms of the cottage, looking for something new and exciting to do. Finding the rooms boring, they scurried into the garden. They quickly jumped up every tree and looked under every stone and around every flower they could find. They sprinted up the hill and ran down to the stream.

"Everything is the same," moaned Nettle. The two squirrels sat down and looked around, waiting for something wonderful to happen. Nothing happened, so they trapesed back to the cottage.

Five minutes later Mrs. Thorn asked them, "What is wrong with you two?" She was trying to spring clean and was beginning to get rather annoyed with the two squirrels, who kept jumping from one side of the room to the other.

"We don't know what to do," sighed Nettle.

"Why don't you run around the garden?" suggested Mrs. Thorn.

"We've already done that," cried Dock.

"Then go to the stream," said Mrs. Thorn.

"We've done that too," replied Nettle, who was now chewing on the leg of Mrs. Thorn's favourite cabinet.

Mrs. Thorn stomped towards Nettle and yanked his tail hard, causing Nettle's mouth to pull away from the cabinet leg. "Well, find something to do that does not involve making my life harder," wailed Mrs. Thorn.

Dock then lay down on his back, and began to throw an acorn up and down with his tail. "What are you doing Mrs. Thorn?" he asked.

"I am spring cleaning," declared Mrs. Thorn. "So, stay out of my way."

"Spring cleaning," repeated Nettle, his excitement growing at the thought.

Nettle began running around Mrs. Thorn and jumping up and down. "Can we help?" asked Nettle enthusiastically.

Mrs. Thorn took a step back, confused by the question, then gathered her composure and replied, "Absolutely not."

Dock had also had a burst of enthusiasm at the mention of spring cleaning, but unlike Nettle, approached Mrs. Thorn a little more carefully. "Under your instructions Mrs. Thorn, we could help you get the spring cleaning done much faster."

This comment took Mrs. Thorn by surprise. Instead of simply saying "no", she started to become a little bit flustered. "Well, I always do the spring cleaning myself. There is really no need."

Nettle opened his mouth and was obviously about to say something far too brash and direct, so Dock quickly cut in.

"It would be our pleasure to help you - especially since you have done it every year without anyone's help."

"Well, that is very nice of you to recognize," said Mrs. Thorn, softly brushing the fur on her face.

Nettle was again about to say something but Dock quickly delivered his final smooth sentence.

"So, what shall we start with?"

Mrs. Thorn led them to the living room and looked down at the tiled floor that was covered with dirt and grime from a long winter spent inside. "If you really want to help me with the spring cleaning, you can start by scrubbing the floor."

"Yippee," cried Nettle.

He was so desperate to do something that he simply leapt down to the floor and began scrubbing with his tail.

"Wait," yelled Mrs. Thorn. "Not with your tail."

Mrs. Thorn waddled over to the cupboard, pulled out a bucket, some cloths, and two bars of herbal soap. "Fill the bucket up at the stream, and then use a cloth and a bar of soap to scrub the floor," explained Mrs. Thorn.

Nettle nodded, grabbed the bucket, and charged toward the stream, pushing Dock out of his way as he went.

Nettle plunged the bucket into the stream and was already racing back up the hill when Dock caught up with him. But as Nettle was running, the bucket of water sloshed backwards and forwards more and more precariously until all of the water sloshed out of the bucket and landed straight onto Dock's chest.

SPLASH.

Dock scowled at Nettle and grabbed the bucket from him. Dock scampered to the stream, carefully re-filled the bucket, and began walking back up the hill. This irritated Nettle, who wanted to get back as quickly as possible. He tried taking the bucket from Dock but instead emptied the entire bucket over his own head.

SPLOSH.

Now Nettle was dripping wet.

The two squirrels scowled at each other for a while, then began arguing, after which they finally agreed that both of them should hold the bucket at the same time. This worked out well, and they eventually managed to set the full bucket of water down in front of the cottage.

However, Nettle was just far too impatient. He wanted to start scrubbing the floor straight away. He ran inside to look at the living room floor, then dragged the bucket into the room and emptied it on to the floor.

SPLASH.

Nettle roared with delight to see the water spilling across the room, but Mrs. Thorn was not happy at all.

"What in woodlands name are you doing?" she barked. "You need the water for the soap. Now dry this water up and go and fetch another bucket full."

Dock started to moan at his brother, but they soon sorted it all out, and they were soon stood in the living room with a fresh bucket of water.

Mrs. Thorn slipped the two bars of soap into the bucket and told them, precisely, what they were to do. She warned them both, especially Nettle, not to do anything silly, and to make sure that they removed all of the dirt off the floor.

The two squirrels nodded obediently, although Nettle found it difficult to stop himself from jumping.

When Mrs. Thorn finally left the room, Nettle let his pent-up energy loose. He dove onto the floor and vigorously began scrubbing.

Dock was enthusiastic, but not quite to the extent that Nettle was. They were both happy to have something different to do but even though it was completely different to anything they had done before, scrubbing a floor is quite a mundane activity, and they quickly became bored.

After a little while Nettle smiled at Dock, who was still scrubbing away.

"I know what you are thinking, Nettle, and you shouldn't."

"But it is so boring," sighed Nettle.

He was now stood up and seemed to be sizing up the room. Dock glanced at him curiously. It was obvious that Nettle had a mischievous idea in his head; it just wasn't obvious what it was exactly.

Nettle scuttled over to the bucket, plunged his paw into it, and pulled out one of the soap bars. He threw it on the floor, backed up a little, and then leapt on to the soap. Suddenly, Nettle went sliding across the room. "Woohoo, soap-boarding," giggled Nettle.

He slid around the room, sending a trail of soapy bubbles up in his wake.

Dock laughed, but his eyes kept flickering to the doorway that Mrs. Thorn had gone through. Dock didn't want to get into trouble, but nor did he want to miss out on what looked like a lot of fun.

"Come on, Dock, what are you waiting for?" cried Nettle.

Dock glanced at the doorway in trepidation, but Nettle's whoops and cries soon brought him to his feet.

Nettle slid over to the bucket and threw the second bar of soap at Dock.

"Come on, give it a go," he laughed.

It didn't take Dock long to forget himself. Both of them zipped around the room in circles, seeing who could slide the fastest and jump the highest.

They soon discovered that they could create huge wobbly bubbles when they turned at high speed, but after trying this a few times, they suddenly crashed into each other, sending their bars of soap skidding away.

Dock and Nettle rubbed their heads and groaned. A few moments later, Grandpa mouse came hobbling into the room.

"Is it lunchtime yet?" he asked out loud.

Dock and Nettle were still sat on the floor, rubbing their heads. They looked over at Grandpa mouse just as he stepped on to both bars of soap.

"Watch out Grandpa," they cried.

It was too late; Grandpa mouse was already sliding across the floor.

"I'm young again," he giggled hysterically.

Dock and Nettle scampered after Grandpa mouse.

"Jump off," they cried.

But Grandpa mouse was now spinning in circles and zigzagging unpredictably around the living room.

When Mrs. Thorn came into the room, she stared, wide-eyed, at Grandpa mouse, who appeared to be gracefully dancing across the room.

"Grab my paw," cried Dock to Grandpa mouse.

Grandpa mouse was still giggling, and instead of reaching out to take Dock's paw, he began flapping his arms about.

"Look, I'm a bird," he cried.

As Grandpa mouse flapped, he turned and slid straight into Mrs. Thorn, sending them both crashing to the ground.

"I always knew I could fly," cried Grandpa mouse with a smile.

Mrs. Thorn glared at Dock and Nettle. Neither squirrel said anything, the glare from Mrs. Thorn said it all. The glare told them to control themselves. The glare told them to calm themselves down. The glare told them to work on their patience. Dock and Nettle soaked up these messages from Mrs. Thorn as they helped Grandpa mouse and Mrs. Thorn back onto their feet.

Dock, who was more embarrassed than Nettle, scurried across the living room floor, doing his best to make the room tidy and presentable, but despite the soap-boarding, or perhaps because of the soap-boarding, the floor was sparkly clean.

When Mrs. Thorn peered down at the floor, her glare slowly transformed into a smile when she realized how clean it was. Nettle had his eyes closed and was waiting for Mrs. Thorn to begin yelling at them, but she didn't.

"Next," began Mrs. Thorn, "you can help me clean out the gutters."

The squirrels cleaned the gutters, and then helped Mrs. Thorn with a whole range of other spring cleaning chores. Nettle still fooled around a lot, but this did not bother Mrs. Thorn too much. She was hesitant to allow the squirrels to help, but she quickly understood that a willing, helpful paw is not one that should be discouraged. Every squirrel and every child possess that wonderful power of helpfulness. If you are a child (or a squirrel), make sure you use this power, and if you are a parent (or a hedgehog), make sure you let them.

Late Spring

Silba's Lair

Be brave, step forward, and use what you have.

Dock and Nettle began their day by picking dandelions. They made their way onto the grassy garden, and ran around happily picking up all these dandelions and placing them in the special backpacks they had made.

There weren't too many dandelions on the grassy garden, but the ones that they found were big and would make for an exciting game. As they were collecting dandelions, Dock found a tiny, shiny bell.

"Wow," he cried, listening to its sharp ring.

"Come on, Dock, let's start," cried Nettle excitedly.

So, Dock stuffed the bell into his pocket and ran back inside with Nettle.

The game they were going to play was called "dandelion shower". One player has to blow the seeds of a dandelion, while the other player has to try and dodge the flying seeds. If the seeds stick to the player's coat who's dodging, then the player who's blowing wins some points.

"That's three points to me," cried Nettle.

"I can only see two seeds," complained Dock.

They were just about to swap when their game was interrupted by Mrs. Thorn.

"I need your help with looking after Grandpa mouse," explained Mrs. Thorn.

"But we are playing dandelion shower," cried Nettle.

Mrs. Thorn just ignored their protests.

"I'm going to the market for berries. I won't be gone very long. Just keep an eye on him and make sure he doesn't go outside," said Mrs. Thorn, as she grabbed a basket.

Grandpa mouse was sat in his favourite chair, reading a book. Well, he was trying to read a book, but he was holding it upside down.

"I can't read mole language," he cried.

Mrs. Thorn scurried out the house with her basket while Grandpa mouse began to stand up and totter around the room.

"Where is my tail?" he muttered, while emptying the cupboards.

Nettle shrugged at Dock.

"Let's continue. He won't go anywhere," said Nettle.

Dock was about to suggest that they should probably wait until Mrs. Thorn returned, but Nettle had already picked up a large dandelion out of his backpack, and blew on it, sending a spiral of seeds zipping through the air.

Dock was agile. He ducked, jumped, twisted and spun all around the room, but he still managed to get covered in dandelion seeds.

"Hahaha," laughed Nettle, as he began counting the seeds. "I win."

Nettle began to pluck the seeds from Dock's coat, but when Nettle tried to count the seeds stuck to Dock's tail, he found Dock's tail straighten in alarm.

"What's wrong?" asked Nettle.

Dock began scurrying around the room. "Grandpa mouse, where is he?" wailed Dock.

As soon as they discovered the front door unbolted and wide open, they both dived outside in a panic.

"Grandpa, Grandpa, where are you?" they screamed.

They scampered around the house, over the house, and up the trees, yelling for their Grandpa, but Grandpa mouse was nowhere in sight.

"What was he looking for when Mrs. Thorn left?" cried Dock, trying to remember the last moments they saw him.

Nettle knocked on his own head like he was knocking a door. "He was looking for his tail."

"That's right," said Dock, with a quick note of triumph in his voice. "But that's not very helpful, he could have gone anywhere."

Dock raised his paws to his forehead and looked right to left. "But at least we know he won't have gone too far," said Nettle hopefully.

This was true, Grandpa mouse was so old that nobody knew how old he was. Even Grandpa mouse didn't know how old he was.

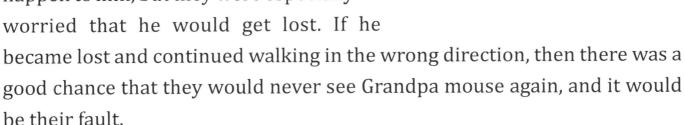

Nevertheless, Dock and Nettle began to shake with worry. Anything could happen to him, but they were especially worried that he would get lost. If he became lost and continued walking in the wrong direction, then there was a good chance that they would never see Grandpa mouse again, and it would be their fault.

There was only one pathway that led away from their cottage, so Dock and Nettle raced along it as fast as they could.

When they came to the cross-path there was still no sign of Grandpa mouse, so they stopped and sniffed around a bit.

The path then split into three different paths. One path led to the market where Mrs. Thorn had gone. The second path led to the coast, and the third path led to a large floral garden.

"Mr. Magpie," cried Dock, pointing up to a tree that held a large nest. "He might have spotted Grandpa." Dock and Nettle cupped their hands and yelled, "Mr. Magpie."

Mr. Magpie had been busy all morning attending to his nest. When he heard the two squirrels yelling, he poked his beak down at them.

"I am extremely busy, what do you want?" he called down.

"Have you seen Grandpa mouse? And if you have, do you know which way he went?"

There was silence, followed by a twig being thrown out of the nest.

"I may have seen him," came Mr. Magpie's smug reply.

Dock and Nettle jumped up in excitement.

"Which way did he go?" they cried.

Mr. Magpie's head once again appeared from over the nest.

"It will cost you," coughed Mr. Magpie.

Mr. Magpie was friendly enough, but he didn't do anything for free. He was obsessed with shiny things. He collected them and used them to decorate his nest, which he was forever pruning and improving.

"Please, Mr. Magpie, just tell us," wailed Nettle.

Mr. Magpie glared down at them indignantly.

"No pay, no say," he squawked, before disappearing once again into his nest.

The two squirrels searched their pockets for something to give Mr. Magpie. Nettle had a half-nibbled acorn and a pebble.

"How about this?" cried Nettle, throwing the pebble up to Mr. Magpie.

There were a few moments silence before the pebble came hurtling back down and smacked Nettle right on the snout.

"This is a pebble," he squawked. "Give me something shiny, and I will tell you where your Grandpa went."

Dock reached into his pocket.

"Of course," he cried. "I found a bell when we were picking dandelions," cried Dock excitedly. He pulled the small bell out of his pocket and threw it up to Mr. Magpie, who caught it in his beak and immediately placed it in his nest.

"Tell us," demanded Dock and Nettle.

Mr. Magpie flew out of his nest and landed on a nearby branch. He cleared his beak and puffed out his chest importantly.

"Your Grandpa walked up the path crying out that he had lost his tail," declared Mr. Magpie.

"Yes, we know that," cried Nettle rather rudely. "Just tell us which way he went."

Dock and Nettle were becoming very anxious. With all the time they had wasted waiting for Mr. Magpie, anything could have happened to Grandpa mouse.

Annoyed with being interrupted, Mr. Magpie flapped his wings and pointed down a fourth overgrown pathway.

"He went that way," squawked Mr. Magpie.

Dock and Nettle froze.

"Are you sure?" muttered Dock, but Mr. Magpie had already flown back into his nest.

The path that Grandpa mouse had taken led to Silba's lair. They would have to hurry if they wanted to bring him back safely. Unless, of course, Silba had already found Grandpa mouse.

Silba was a snake, an old adder, that lived in the darkest part of the woodland. Everyone knew that they should keep well away from Silba, who, in return for not being disturbed, would hunt creatures outside the woodland border. Unless any creatures wandered knowingly or unknowingly into her lair.

Dock and Nettle hoped that Silba was not home. If she was home, then they hoped that she wasn't hungry. If she was hungry, then they had little else they could hope for.

Dock and Nettle stood there frozen, they didn't dare move on to the path in case, by taking just one step on to the path, they drew Silba toward them. All of a sudden, Dock took a big gulp, stepped forward, and then looked at Nettle.

"We have to. If we don't then Grandpa will be gone and we will regret this moment forever."

Nettle, encouraged by Dock's bravery, tried his best to put his fear behind him. Dock was right, if they didn't try and find Grandpa, they would regret it. Nettle wanted to say that perhaps Grandpa may already be lost, but didn't voice it, Dock's bravery was contagious, and soon they took the plunge and scurried down the dark, creepy path.

They both ran as fast as their little legs would take them. It was only when they came to a part of the woodland that was truly frightening, did they begin to slow down.

The woodland was ordinarily filled with vegetation, greenery and leaves, but this place was the complete opposite. The ground was barren and broken. Dead plants and broken branches littered the floor. There was a strong, pungent smell, which smelt like a mixture of rot, mould and decay, and flies infested the air, buzzing in swarms that rose and fell like the waves of the sea. Even the trees seemed frightening. They loomed over Dock and Nettle as if they were waiting for the squirrels to step in front of them so that they could crash down and trap them.

"Grandpa," hissed Dock and Nettle. "Where are you?"

The brothers were becoming more and more frightened by the second, and began to feel their courage leaking from them like sap from a tree, but despite how scared they were, they bravely moved forward through the thicket of scary trees. As they reached the middle of the thicket, they spotted Grandpa mouse. He was slowly shuffling towards them. The reason he was moving so slowly was that he had something long, heavy, and translucent slumped over his shoulder.

"Grandpa," shouted Dock and Nettle, much louder than they should have.

Grandpa mouse looked up at them, and realizing who they were, waved.

"I found my tail," he cried triumphantly.

Dock and Nettle bounded up to Grandpa mouse.

"That isn't your tail," gasped Dock. "That's Silba's skin."

On his search for a tail, Grandpa mouse had come across Silba's skin (the dry, flaky skin that the snake sheds at the end of every season).

"Come on, Grandpa," cried Nettle, grabbing Grandpa mouse's paw. "We shouldn't be here. We have to leave."

Dock grabbed one paw while Nettle grabbed the other. Together they began to pull Grandpa mouse back the way they had come.

"Are we going to the beach?" cried Grandpa mouse.

Then, Grandpa mouse began whooping in delight.

"Be quiet," hissed Nettle. But it was already too late.

The two squirrels froze. Their tails tensed, and their eyes flickered across the undergrowth. Silba had heard them, and now she was slithering towards them through the undergrowth. Within moments, Silba emerged from the bushes, she coiled her body and raised her head in the air. Her tongue flickered out from her mouth as she spoke.

"Nicccccce of you to drop by," she hissed.

"I found my tail," cheered Grandpa mouse.

"W..w..we are sorry," stammered Dock.

"It was Grandpa," added Nettle quickly. "He wandered in here by mistake. We will leave right away." Nettle pulled Grandpa mouse's paw, forcing all three of them into a slow walk.

Silba quickly slithered her way in front of them. "Sssso sssssoon?" she hissed. "But we haven't had dinner yet." Silba began slithering closer and closer to them.

"Lovely," cried Grandpa mouse. "What are we having?"

Silba slithered closer, while Dock and Nettle took frantic steps back, pulling Grandpa mouse back with them.

"What do we do now?" whispered Dock to Nettle, his voice barely audible.

Nettle looked around for anything that might help them. They couldn't fight the snake, nor could they run from her without being struck down. All they had with them was their backpacks. Nettle's fur stood on end. "We have the dandelions," whispered Nettle enthusiastically. "Quickly, get one out of your backpack." Nettle reached over his shoulder and pulled one out while Dock did the same. The three of them were quickly stepping backwards, as Silba slithered faster towards them.

"Okay," said Nettle, "on the count of three."

Sensing that something was about to happen, Silba began to slither forward even faster.

"One," said Nettle, but Silba had already raised her head, ready to lunge at them.

Dock and Nettle blew on their dandelions, sending a shower of seeds swirling in the air.

Silba half lunged towards them, but the swirling, floating seeds confused her. She became disorientated and began moving her head from side to side and up and down. "Quickly, run," cried Nettle. Still holding Grandpa mouse's paws, they jumped over Silba and out of the thicket of trees. They tried to sprint along the path, but Grandpa mouse slowed them down. A minute later they heard an ominous hissing sound behind them that was beginning to grow louder and louder. Dock bravely pushed Nettle and Grandpa mouse forward while he turned and pulled two dandelions out of his backpack.

"Keep going," cried Dock.

Nettle, who was in tears, stumbled on with Grandpa mouse, his eyes fixed on the path ahead, but his ears were focused on the wild spitting and hissing sounds that were happening behind them. When they finally reached the cross path, Nettle threw Grandpa mouse to the ground and turned back towards the pathway. "Dock," he cried desperately. He couldn't believe. He wouldn't believe that his brother wasn't coming back. It was because of Dock's bravery that Grandpa mouse was found. It was because of Dock's bravery that they were now safe. He has to come back, willed Nettle. Two butterflies floated across the path, then all of a sudden Dock appeared in the pathway. Nettle rushed up to Dock and gave him the most tremendous of hugs. "Well done, Dock," cried Nettle.

As they walked more slowly back to the cottage, they began to think up a story they could tell Mrs. Thorn. They decided on a story that involved all three of them looking for dandelions, but Dock and Nettle hadn't noticed the snakeskin that was still tied around Grandpa mouse's shoulder. Mrs. Thorn spotted this immediately.

"Why is there a snake's tail wrapped around Grandpa mouse?" she pointed out.

Grandpa mouse, who had almost fallen asleep on the walk back from Mr. Magpie's nest, suddenly perked up. "I found my tail," he yelled enthusiastically.

Dock and Nettle looked at each other nervously and then relayed the whole story to Mrs. Thorn. They had expected her to yell and shout, call them irresponsible and careless, but instead she gasped and even clapped when they told her how they blew the dandelion seed at Silba's face.

"You were both very brave squirrels," announced Mrs. Thorn. "And you," she gestured at Grandpa mouse.

"Live to see another day," said Mrs. Thorn. Grandpa mouse untied the translucent snakeskin from around his shoulder and looked at it. "This isn't my tail," he cried angrily. "Where is my tail?" Dock bounded up to Grandpa mouse and affectionately lifted Grandpa's tail and placed it in his paw.

"Oh yes," giggled Grandpa mouse. "The things we most need are always close at paw," he said wisely. And indeed they are.

Being brave with others is much easier than being brave by yourself, but even with others, someone has to take that first step. When that step is taken, the rest will follow more easily. It was Dock that took that first step, but that does not mean that Nettle's steps were unimportant. Nettle blew the dandelions that allowed them to escape, and Dock built upon that bravery further still towards the end of their terrible trial. But please remember Grandpa mouse's words. Everything that we need, we already have, no matter what the problem may be, no matter the difficulty. Be brave, step forward, and use what you have.

Early Summer

A Day at the Races

Actions speak louder than words.

"It's today," yelled Nettle.

He jumped out of his bed and leapt on to Dock's bed. Dock was still trying to get some more sleep, but Nettle was shaking him like the branch of a tree.

"Wake up, wake up," cried Nettle.

Dock began to moan, but then realized what day it was and jumped up from his bed.

"It's race day," cried Dock.

Nettle drew back the curtains and threw open the window, sending beams of light spilling into the room.

"There isn't a moment to lose," cried Nettle.

Dock and Nettle were both so excited because today was the woodland hare race.

All the hares from far and wide, gathered to take part in the race. Every single hare, old or young, fast or slow, would join in the race. For most of the hares, it was a fun tradition, but for some hares the race was a matter of pride. Whoever won the race would be known as "hurdle hare", the fastest and most agile hare around. For that is what it takes to win the race - speed and agility.

The hares would have to race across meadows, jump over logs, zigzag between bushes, and make sure that they didn't slip into the mud.

However, the best thing about the race was that all of the other animals in the woodland could also enjoy the spectacle. Every friendly creature from miles around would gather at the highest point of the woodland, a rocky crag that looks down over the final section of the racecourse.

In the weeks leading up to this year's race, hares could be spotted throughout the woodland, training for the competition. Two hares in particular could be spotted nearly every day, and they didn't just train. They etched lifelike sketches of themselves into the trees and bushes, and as race day loomed closer, they began holding small rallies to gain more and more supporters. These two fine, athletic specimens were Linda and Ronald, and these were the two hares that Dock and Nettle had tipped to win the race. Dock was supporting "Leaping Linda", as she had become known. While Nettle was supporting "Racing Ronald".

Dock and Nettle both gulped down their breakfasts without even looking at it, and urged Mrs. Thorn to hurry up.

"We don't want to be late," they cried.

They pushed Mrs. Thorn out of the door and pulled her along the path.

"I think Linda is going to win," cried Dock.

He then raced ahead on the path shouting, "Leaping Linda."

Nettle scoffed. "Don't be ridiculous - Linda won't win. The winner will be Ronald. He is much faster than Linda."

Nettle sprinted up the path as if to somehow prove that Ronald would beat Linda. But as Nettle went sprinting up the path, Dock stuck his leg out and tripped Nettle up, who went sliding across the floor headfirst.

Dock giggled, "Linda would have jumped over that easily."

Nettle scowled at Dock, but luckily Mrs. Thorn quickly intervened, putting an end to their impending fight.

"I don't think either of them will win," declared Mrs. Thorn.

Dock and Nettle stared at Mrs. Thorn in amazement.

"Are you joking?" cried Nettle.

"There are no other hares that want to win as much as they do," cried Dock.

"They are far too boastful and sure of themselves," explained Mrs. Thorn. "In a race, you never know what will happen, anyone can win."

The two squirrels frowned.

"No way," said Nettle. "Ronald won't lose."

Mrs. Thorn was about to explain further, but the path they were walking on began to merge with the other paths, and within moments they were joined by an array of other creatures who were also making their way to watch the race.

"I think Linda will win," cried a young mouse, as the climb upwards began to get steeper. "I saw her training, she was leaping over three logs at a time, she's amazing."

A young hedgehog disagreed. "No way. Linda has a good leap, but she doesn't have the speed of Ronald."

Dock and Nettle were about to add their opinion to the discussion, but before they could do so, they found they had reached the top of the crag. The crag was bustling with activity. There were families laying out picnics. Birds were zipping through the air, and there was even a great big badger performing tricks for the youngsters.

"For my next performance," cried the badger. "I need four hedgehog volunteers."

There was a squeal of excitement from the hedgehogs in the crowd, and a flurry of paws shot straight up into the air. The hedgehog that Dock and Nettle had met on the walk to the crag also had her paw in the air. She was jumping up and down furiously.

"Me, pick me, I'm the best with tricks," she squealed. The badger looked out at the crowd and chose four hedgehogs, completely dismissing the jumpy, boastful hedgehog.

Dock and Nettle watched as she scowled and stomped off angrily.

"Why didn't he choose her?" whispered Nettle.

Dock shrugged and continued to watch the badger.

When the volunteers had settled themselves in front of him, he slowly looked up at the crowd and began a dramatic introduction.

"I must ask the audience for complete and utter silence during this trick."

He took a couple of paces towards the audience and then stood over his volunteers.

"The four of you must curl up in a ball and sleep."

The badger pulled out a pocket watch from his waistcoat and dangled it in front of the four hedgehogs. He swung it from side to side like a pendulum. After a couple of swings, the badger suddenly clicked his paws and slipped the watch back into his pocket. The four hedgehogs dropped to the floor and curled themselves up.

"Silence now," whispered the badger to the audience.

The badger carefully scooped up the four prickly hedgehogs in his paws.

After a few moments of slowly bouncing them on his knees, the badger suddenly threw the hedgehogs, one by one, into the air. Then, one by one, he caught them in his other paw before sending them flying into the air again. He was juggling with the hedgehogs.

The crowd gasped and then clapped as the badger juggled. Then, slowly and carefully, the badger, caught each hedgehog and laid each one delicately on the floor.

"Observe," he cried, showing the audience his paws. "I am unharmed."

He then clapped loudly two times, and the four hedgehogs woke from their slumber and the crowd burst into cheers.

"He doesn't even have a scratch," came a cry from in front of Dock and Nettle.

The clapping was soon silenced by a big flock of birds who descended upon the small crowd.

"Quick," they twittered.

"The race is about to start." All of the creatures quickly ran up to the highest point of the crag, which promised the best possible view, not of the beginning of the race, but the end of the race. For the beginning of the race the crowd would have to rely on the twittering of two birds that had taken it upon themselves to act as commentators. The only problem was that the two birds could not agree with what was happening.

"They're off," cried the blue tit. The crowd cheered, but the cheer was quickly quietened by the great tit.

"No, they are not," squawked the great tit. "They're not even moving."

The blue tit then squinted, trying to get a better look. "Oh yeah, you're right," he squawked. "They're not off."

"Well, they are now," retorted the great tit, fluttering down and pecking the blue tit on the top of his head.

The blue tit swooped up. "Yes, they are off," chattered the blue tit more loudly.

The animals on the ground chattered and cheered, and for the next five minutes listened intently to the commentary from the blue tit and great tit.

From the commentary, the animals on the ground understood that at the front of the race there was a battle between the two favourites, Leaping Linda and Racing Ronald, with the rest of the hares far behind these two.

When the two leading hares burst out onto the meadow, there came a sudden chatter from the crowd as everyone stopped listening to the blue tit and great tit and began their own commentary.

The two leading hares were the two favourites, Linda and Ronald. They both glanced up at the crag, fully aware of the audience that was watching them. They pushed their chests out and stretched their legs in response to the chorus of cries that were floating down to them.

"LINDA," cried Dock.

"RONALD," bellowed Nettle even louder.

The two leading hares were half-way through the meadow now. At the end of the meadow they would have to jump a hedgerow and then run through another meadow filled with pools of mud and logs. They would then exit that field and begin their ascent of the crag. The first to reach the top would be crowned "hurdle hare". At present, Linda was leading, but with no obstacles in front of them, Ronald quickly reached his top speed and began to edge ahead of her.

"Woohoo," cried Nettle. "Go, Ronald."

Ronald quickly shot ahead, but as they got closer to the hedgerow, he began to hesitate and stumble, as he tried to decide the best place to jump over the hedgerow.

Linda took advantage of Ronald's hesitation by striding forward and leaping over both Ronald and the hedgerow.

Dock jumped up excitedly.

"Leaping Linda, Leaping Linda," he chanted.

Nettle groaned as he watched Ronald stumble and crash into the hedgerow.

"Come on, Ronald. Get up," cried Nettle.

Linda had already landed gracefully in the second meadow and quickly glanced back to look at what had happened to Ronald. This was a huge mistake because as she glanced back, she failed to notice a large puddle of mud in front of her. When she eventually looked forward and saw where she was going, her front paws were already sliding in the mud. She tried to jump clear, but she was uncontrollably sliding forward now. Her body was twisting this way and that way, and within a few moments, she rolled and collided with a log. By the time Linda managed to get up and begin running again, Ronald was once again by her side. They were both hopping from side to side, turning and leaping, so as to avoid the big pools of mud. When they eventually reached the end of the meadow Linda, who was covered in mud, and Ronald, who was punctured with thorns, both turned to face the last challenge – climbing the crag. As the two hares took their first hops up the crag, the crowd rumbled with excitement. Linda seemed to leap higher than Ronald while Ronald seemed to be running faster than Linda, but neither of them seemed to be leading. With neither of them winning and both of them beginning to run out of steam, they started to become more and more desperate. At first, they both began softly knocking into each other, each trying to cause the other one to stumble just enough to allow the other one to win, but as they neared the finish line they were both still neck and neck. They flung themselves at each other harder and harder, and then with one almighty crash, they both smashed into each other at the same time. The crash sent both of them smashing into the ground, where they slid and crashed into a large rock. There was stunned silence from the crowd, who was desperately urging their favourites on. Linda and Ronald were done for. They looked up at the crowd, with their mouths hanging open. Then they both tried to stand, but tripped and stumbled back onto the floor. The crowd all groaned, then the blue tit and then the great tit began twittering excitedly. Everyone shifted their gaze away from Ronald and Linda, because another hare was now racing up to the top of the crag. It was Benjamin, a hare that no one knew the name of. He hopped up past the two hares and glanced at them as he did so. Linda and Ronald tried to jump up when they saw him pass them, but in doing so they both tangled their legs up and smacked into the rock face again.

"No way," cried Dock and Nettle at the same time.

At first, the crowd had gone quiet with shock, but now, as Benjamin edged closer to the finish line at the top of the crag, everyone began to clap and cheer for the hare that everyone knew was about to become the "hurdle hare". As the day finished and the crowds headed home, Dock and Nettle still found it difficult to accept that Linda and Ronald had lost the race.

"I told you that neither of them would win," said Mrs. Thorn knowingly.

"But they were the best," cried Dock and Nettle in protest.

"They were the best," agreed Mrs. Thorn.

"But neither of them won," said Mrs. Thorn.

Neither squirrel had an answer to this statement and instead listened as Mrs. Thorn continued to speak. "Actions speak louder than words, dear squirrels. Many who say they can, think they can, but don't know they can. Whereas those who know they can, think they can, but don't say they can. Does that make sense?"

Dock and Nettle shook their heads and were about to listen to Mrs. Thorn explain more when they caught sight of Linda and Ronald.

Linda was still covered in mud and Ronald's fur was still punctured with thorns. They were arguing with each other and were trying to convince the dispersing crowd who was the faster hare, despite the fact that neither of them had finished the race. Their cries for attention were soon lost on the crowd when the humble, but victorious, Benjamin appeared.

"Look! It's the hurdle hare," cried an excited mouse.

Benjamin was quickly lifted into the air by the happy crowd. This was his rightful moment, and he deserved every second of it.

In a race of any sort, confidence is key, but respect also plays an important role, because in the end, results are results, and nothing can change the result. Dock and Nettle were easily dragged into the leaping Linda and racing Ronald mania but thankfully, I think they understood towards the end – actions speak louder than words.

Late Summer

Questions

Curiosity killed the cat, but what will it do to two young squirrels?

Dock and Nettle had been following Mrs. Thorn all morning, their mouths filled with a multitude of questions. "Where does rain come from?" asked Dock, jumping up and down.

"Why is the sky blue?" asked Nettle, swinging his tail from side to side.

"Where does the sun go?" bellowed Dock, frustrated that he didn't know the answer.

Mrs. Thorn brushed them both aside irritably. "Questions, questions, questions," she sighed. "I am far too busy to be answering all of these questions. Go ask Grandpa mouse."

So, Dock and Nettle ran up to Grandpa mouse, who was sat in the garden soaking up the sun. "

We have questions," cried Dock and Nettle excitedly, as they ran out of the house.

"Oh, goodie. I love a quiz," said Grandpa mouse.

"Why is the sky blue?" asked Nettle quickly.

Grandpa mouse opened his mouth and let out an array of thinking sounds before blurting out an answer. "Because of blueberries," said Grandpa mouse.

Nettle frowned while Dock bounded in with his own question.

"What makes the rain?"

Grandpa mouse slapped his paws together and bobbed his head up and down. "Bird pee," he cried.

It was Dock's turn to frown now.

Finally, the two squirrels looked at each other before asking their final question. "Where does the sun go?"

This time Grandpa mouse smiled. "Well, that's easy. The sun goes home." Dock and Nettle looked at each other and sighed. "Well," said Grandpa mouse, "did I get them right?"

They returned to Mrs. Thorn and once again pushed her for some answers, but instead of answering their questions she pushed them out of the door, insisting that they go and find the answers for themselves. Dock and Nettle scrambled to the top of the hill that overlooks their cottage.

"Where can we find the answers?" sighed Nettle.

Dock lay down on the grass and stared up at the sky. "There is something that each of our questions have in common," said Dock slowly.

"What's that?" asked Nettle.

The sun is in the sky, the rain falls from the sky, and the sky... is in the sky," said Dock. "If only we could go to the sky, I am sure we would find our answers there."

This sparked an idea that caused Nettle to jump up with glee. "Go to the sky," he repeated. "Of course." Nettle climbed up the trunk and along the branch of a nearby tree.

"Don't be silly," said Dock. "We can't go to the sky."

Nettle threw an acorn down at Dock, who was still lying down on the ground. The acorn smacked him on the head and caused him to jump up and wave his paw at Nettle angrily. "We can't go. But they can," said Nettle, pointing at some birds that were zipping from tree to tree.

"Can we ask you some questions?" cried Dock and Nettle, as they scrambled up the oak tree that overlooked their home. Unfortunately, birds are very busy creatures, and not one of them gave the two squirrels a passing glance. When both Dock and Nettle jumped on the branch, they were hoping to perch on it in an effort to attract the attention of a passing sparrow. However, they both missed their footing and tumbled off the branch and landed on the ground.

"Ouch," cried Dock and Nettle, rubbing their heads. As they picked themselves up from the floor, Dock noticed something glinting in the bushes. "Oh, look, buttons," cried Dock.

Dock pulled out four beautiful brass buttons from the bushes.

The buttons sparked an idea in Nettle's mind, and he quickly reached out and snatched one from Dock's paw.

"Hey, that's mine. Give it back," cried Dock. "I found it first." But Nettle was already racing along the woodland path away from Dock. "Give me my button back," cried Dock, chasing after Nettle. It took Dock a while to catch up with Nettle, but when he eventually did, he found Nettle calling up to a tree.

"Mr. Magpie. Are you there?" cried Nettle. The black and white magpie jumped up to the edge of his nest and peered down at them. The Magpie's beady black eyes spied the button in Nettle's paw. "We have a question," called Nettle, throwing the button up.

Mr. Magpie jumped out of his nest and plucked the button out of the air. "What do you want to know?" asked the Magpie.

"We want to know why the sky is blue, what makes the rain, and where the sun goes," explained Nettle.

Mr. Magpie craned his head and then opened his beak. "That is not one question, that is three questions. If you wish me to give you three answers, then you must give me three payments." He then fluttered his wings and said, "No pay, no say."

Nettle sighed and then looked across at Dock, who was trying to catch his breath. "Give him two more of your buttons," ordered Nettle.

Dock scowled and refused, but after a little bit of coaxing from Nettle, Dock finally succumbed and pulled out two more of the buttons from his pocket. Nettle threw the buttons up and then demanded the answers from Mr. Magpie.

The magpie squawked, flew to a different branch, and then ceremoniously announced. "I don't know."

"What do you mean you don't know?" cried Dock angrily. "I've just given you three of my buttons. Give them back if you don't have the answers."

Mr. Magpie coughed indignantly. "If you would please let me continue." He jumped across to another branch and puffed out his chest. "I do know a bird that knows the answers to all three of your questions," he squawked. "She is the wisest of all birds. Her name is Dara, and she can be found in the great oak, just a wing flap away from the last tree of the forest."

Dock and Nettle opened their mouths to ask another question, but the rude magpie quickly cut in before they could do so.

"No pay, no say," he said and then flapped his wings and disappeared into his nest. Dock and Nettle had many more questions, but they didn't want to ask Mr. Magpie. His price was far too expensive, so instead, they began scurrying toward the part of the woodland they believed Mr. Magpie was talking about. They made their way along the path, up the crag, through the rabbit meadows and into the final border of trees that mark the boundary of the entire woodland. When they arrived at the final border of trees, they looked out across the fields, and right in front of them was a lone oak tree.

"There," cried Nettle. "It's that one."

As they began to creep out of the woodland borders, they hesitated. They both knew that they weren't supposed to leave the woodland. Mrs. Thorn constantly told them how dangerous the world was outside their small corner of the woodland. "It's just there," said Nettle, trying to build their confidence. "What could possibly go wrong?"

Nettle led the way, scampering from the trees to the field of Barley. Dock reluctantly followed, and together they raced through the long reeds of grain.

The grains of Barley made a terrific whizzing sound as they ran through it. Dock and Nettle soon lost their nervousness and began racing up and down the rows of Barley. They played tag, and then started leaping up as if they were fish in a stream. While they were leaping they remembered why they had come into the field in the first place.

"The oak tree is this way," cried Dock, jumping up to check the direction they should be going.

As they got closer to the tree, the Barley began to thin out, and the sheer size of the oak tree was revealed to them. It was enormous. Bigger than any other tree they had seen inside the woodland.

Dock and Nettle then began to wonder whether they should climb the tree and search for Dara, or whether they should announce themselves while they were on the ground. In the end, they decided it would be more respectful to call out while they were on the ground.

Nettle nudged Dock to make the first call, who nudged Nettle back. But neither of them had to make the first call because Dara was perched on one of the oaks higher branches, her head cocking from side to side.

"May I help you?" said Dara.

Dock and Nettle jumped in fright, and stared up at the bird with a mixture of interest and awe.

Nettle smiled at Dara, and waited for the bird to show some sort of friendly response, but Dara simply cocked her head again and waited.

"W-Well," stammered Nettle. "We have some questions. Mr. Magpie said that you would know the answers to them."

Dara, with a speed that stunned the two squirrels, swooped down to a different branch.

"Mr. Magpie," tutted Dara. "What a silly, foolish bird. But I thank him all the same for sending you my way."

There were a few moments silence in which Dock and Nettle tried to decipher the meaning of what Dara had just said.

"I am sure your questions are very important," cooed Dara, as she jumped down again.

"Yes," agreed Nettle.

Who was glad that someone was finally taking an interest in their questions.

Nettle stood a little straighter and listed out the three questions to Dara.

Dara sat there, unblinking, and listened intently to the questions that Nettle asked. She swooped down again and then opened her beak.

"The answer to each of your questions is the same," announced Dara.

"Really?" asked Dock a little nervously. He was starting to feel that something about this creature was not quite right. Why did she keep getting closer to them, and why wasn't she blinking?

Dock thought for a moment and then realized in alarm what they were talking to.

"Don't look at her eyes. She's an owl," whispered Dock to Nettle.

Dara cocked her head.

"Why don't you want to look at my eyes?" squawked Dara a little aggressively.

Dock froze. How on earth did she hear that, even Nettle had struggled to hear his whisper.

Dara swooped down one more branch and continued as if nothing had happened.

"Yes, the answer to each of your questions is the same."

There was another long silence.

"Soooo," said Nettle softly, trying to think of how they could get away. "What is the answer?"

Dara flapped her wings and flew gracefully around the tree.

"I have flown to the sun, I have flown through the rain, and I have even flown beyond the sky."

Dara flapped her wings softly and looked up.

"Darkness," she screeched.

"Darkness," repeated Nettle, mulling the answer over and completely forgetting that he wanted to run away.

He felt sure that the answers should be more fantastic, more amazing and bright. Dock no longer cared about the questions anymore and was tugging at Nettle's paw and pulling him back towards the field. "Yes... darkness," concluded Dara, as she jumped down onto the ground with a thud. Nettle now understood that this was a bird that they should not have come so close to. She was huge. Her eyes were almost hypnotic and her claws, which until now neither of them had noticed, were sickeningly long and sharp. Her eyes seemed to grow larger as if she were trying to pull the squirrels closer to her with only her eyes. "Come, and I will show you the darkness," she cooed softly. "Beyond the sky, where the rain comes from, and where the sun calls it home." Now that Dara had landed on the ground, the two brothers suddenly noticed things they had failed to notice while craning their necks up at the tree. The ground was littered with bones, animal bones of every size and shape. Their eyes widened almost as much as the owl's. They both began moving backwards even faster now, while Dara continued to hop towards them. "Come, let me show you," she squawked. Her talons were now punching into the ground every time she hopped, throwing up huge clumps of dirt. Tired of waiting, Dara jumped up into the air, spread her two wings out, and dived at Dock and Nettle. Dock and Nettle jumped out of the way just in time. Dara's massive talons smashed into the ground, sending dirt and pebbles flying everywhere. "Come," screeched Dara.

Nettle quickly came to his senses, grabbed Dock's paw, and pulled him into the long sea of Barley. Behind them they heard the beating of wings and the swooshing of wind as Dara pushed herself up into the air.

"Run," cried Nettle.

They both ran as fast as they could through the long thickets of grain.

"We don't know which way we are going," hissed Dock.

They stopped and listened. They could hear the beating of wings and knew that Dara was close by, searching them out.

"We have to jump," hissed Nettle. "We jump, and then run as fast as we can to the woodland."

Nettle then looked at Dock and counted down.

"Three, two, one."

Both of them leapt up into the air as high as they could. As they rose into the air, a loud screech could be heard behind them as Dara's big telescopic eyes locked on to them.

Fortunately, Dock and Nettle had spotted the tree line, and even in mid-air began running forwards. With their hearts pounding and legs racing they charged forward, but within a few moments, they heard the ominous sound of rushing wind. They both looked up and saw Dara plunging down on top of them, her talons reaching at them desperately. The two brothers dived out of the way, a few moments later they were sprayed with dirt from Dara's talons piercing into the earth. They quickly jumped into the air again and headed for the forest. They were so close to the forest now, but Dara was also close behind them. She dived a further two times, her great big talons squirming to catch hold of the squirrels, but Dock and Nettle were just agile enough to dodge out of the way, and as they did so they got closer to the woodland edge, to safety, and home. But Dara wasn't about to give up, she dived at them again. After the spray of dirt and pebbles had settled, Nettle discovered that he was trapped. "I'm stuck," cried Nettle.

Nettle was on his knees with his paws wrapped around his leg which had become trapped in a hole.

Dock scampered back and began pulling at his brother's leg, trying with all his might to break him free. Nettle's leg was slowly coming out of the hole, but not fast enough.

Above them they saw Dara now confidently flapping her wings, watching them and teasing them. She flapped lower and lower, until she hovered directly above them both.

"Come, my little squirrels, I will show you the darkness."

Dock had given up trying to pull Nettle loose and stared up at the owl in terror.

"We don't want to go to the darkness," cried Dock.

Dock's eyes suddenly twitched involuntarily. Sunlight was shining on his face, but not from the sky - it was reflecting from something on the floor.

The button that Dock had found, the last button left after giving the rest to Mr. Magpie, had fallen out of his pocket. With no other ideas at hand, Dock quickly picked up the button and threw it at Dara as hard as he could. It was the right thing to do. Dara flapped up suddenly in shock when the flashing, shiny button shot up at her. This bought Dock and Nettle some time, but not enough. Nettle's leg was shifting out of the hole, but he was still trapped, and now Dara was angry. She dived down at them once again, her talons aiming at Dock and Nettle like spears. Dock closed his eyes, hoping the end would be fast. As he did so, he could see only darkness, and hear only the rushing of air and the beating of wings. Dock braced himself, soon he was being pushed from side to side as the wind grew stronger and stronger. He then fell to the floor from the force of the wind. Dock opened his eyes, and saw a massive flock of magpies, at least twenty of them, including Mr. Magpie, above him. They were fighting for the shiny button. The button itself was tumbling through the air. One magpie would catch it in its beak and then another magpie would lunge in and force the button free, then another magpie would catch the button, and so on and so on. However, Dock could see Dara circling above all of them, trying desperately to fly her way through the group of magpies. Dock grabbed Nettle, and with a humongous heave pulled his leg free of the hole. A few moments later, they dived out of the field of Barley and into the safety of the woodland once more. When Dock and Nettle arrived home, they remained silent for the rest of the day. They didn't dare speak a word. When they closed their eyes, all they could see were Dara's great big eyes staring back at them. They felt almost naked, as if Dara could see what they were doing and hear everything they were saying.

When Mrs. Thorn found them curled up in a corner of the room, she frowned at them. "What in woodlands name is wrong with you two?" she laughed. "Ahhh, I know," she cried. "You found the answers to your questions, didn't you?"

Dock and Nettle looked up at Mrs. Thorn as if they were seeing her for the very first time and nodded their heads.

"Darkness," whispered Nettle.

"Darkness?" repeated Mrs. Thorn. "Who told you that?" Dock and Nettle didn't dare utter the name, and instead looked down at the floor.

Mrs. Thorn thought it was the answer "darkness" that was troubling them both. She had no idea of the ordeal they had just gone through, and she certainly wouldn't have been happy to hear about it. She then gave Dock and Nettle the best words she could muster. "It does not matter where the sun goes, or what makes the rain, nor why the sky is blue," explained Mrs. Thorn. "All that matters, is that it happens. We must be thankful for the life we have."

Dock and Nettle had been shivering and shaking but now began to warm up and lighten.

By the end of the day they were playing and joking once more, although it might be a while before they start seeking the answers to any new questions they have.

Well, I am very glad that Dock and Nettle are safe and well, but I am equally glad that they found the answers to their questions. Without curiosity, there is so much about this world that we will miss out on.

Early Autumn

Night Walk

Look up once in a while, so that you know you are going the right way.

"Make sure you are back home by supper time," cried Mrs. Thorn to Dock and Nettle.

The two squirrels looked back, nodded their heads, and grinned as they went racing outside. It had been raining non-stop for the past week, which meant that Dock and Nettle had been stuck inside the cottage. Now that the rain had eased, the two squirrels were itching to stretch their legs and sniff their snouts.

"Look," cried Nettle. Nettle was pointing at a group of snails. The constant rain had brought the snails out of their hiding places, and they were now sliming across the ground in a long line.

"Where are they going?" asked Dock. Nettle edged closer to one of the larger snails and very carefully and very tenderly picked it up. The snail squirmed around and then disappeared into its shell.

"Where are you going?" asked Nettle, speaking very loudly. Nettle peered into the shell and was about to repeat the question when the snail, who obviously didn't like being disturbed in this way, suddenly burst back out of its shell. Nettle dropped the shell in shock and took a few steps back.

"Look," said Dock. "There's a long line of them." Dock bounded along the garden and discovered that the snails were slithering in a line, following each other.

Dock and Nettle ran beside the long procession of snails. They wondered where they were going and what they were doing.

Dock and Nettle's curiosity only increased the further along the trail of snails they went. The line of snails seemed endless. At first, they followed the trail along the path, which led them up to the cross-roads tree where Mr. Magpie lived. After that, the trail of snails led out into the undergrowth. Dock and Nettle looked at each other hesitantly, but it was only a momentary glance. They soon dived into the undergrowth, and carried on trotting past the line of snails, wondering when the front of the procession would reveal itself. But the line was endless. They scampered through bushes, scrambled through ditches and jumped over logs, but they still didn't reach the front of the procession. The more time that passed, the more determined Dock and Nettle became. They simply had to find out what was at the front of this long line of snails. Dock and Nettle looked at nothing else but the snails. To begin with, they thought that the snails were all alike, but they began to notice that the patterns on each of the snail's shells were all different. It was only when the fading light made it difficult for them to see the patterns on the snails shells that Dock and Nettle began to take in their surroundings.

"Do you know where we are?" asked Dock frightfully.

Nettle had stopped and was looking up, down, left and right. He wrapped his tail around his body protectively. "I – I – I don't know," he stammered. Dock and Nettle didn't recognize any part of the woodland that they now found themselves in, and the light was fading fast. Soon the forest would be enveloped in darkness.

"What do we do?" cried Dock frantically.

Nettle shivered at the thought of being lost in the woodland. Both Dock and Nettle had grown up hearing stories of the terrible creatures that stalked the forest at night, foxes and ferrets, even wolves - those legendary creatures that send ear-splitting howls echoing through the woodland. Dock and Nettle had never heard a howl before, in fact, no one had ever heard a howl, but right there in the darkening forest, Dock and Nettle felt that they would hear a howl at any moment.

Nettle quickly realized something. How could they be so stupid?

"We just go back the way we came," cried Nettle triumphantly.

"B-B-But we don't know where we are," stammered Dock.

"We can follow the snails back," said Nettle confidently.

Dock brightened at this idea, and looked down for the snails. It was an excellent idea, except the fading light was making it difficult for them to see anything.

"Where are they?" cried Dock.

Nettle squinted at the ground, but it was of no use. The light had already been sucked out of the woodland. It was now becoming difficult to see their own tails, never mind a small snail.

The two squirrels hugged, and wrapped their tails around each other. They felt completely helpless. They trembled and thought about Mrs. Thorn. What would she be thinking now? Would she be walking through the forest looking for them? What if she got hurt? Their minds raced from one terror to another, when suddenly, a little way ahead of them, a light began to twinkle. It wasn't a very bright light, just slightly bigger and brighter than a star in the sky, but it was definitely a light.

Dock and Nettle automatically moved towards it. The closer they got, the more excited and anxious they became. "How do we know it's safe?" whispered Dock.

"Well, what could be dangerous about it?" whispered Nettle.

"It might be a fox or a ferret," whispered Dock hurriedly.

Despite their conversation, they still edged closer and closer. They began to see an outline of a small house. From what they could see of it in the gloom, it looked well built, with strong, painted walls, a thatched roof and latticed windows. If Dock and Nettle had seen this house anywhere else they would have assumed it to be completely normal, but finding it in this wild area of the wood unsettled them. Something just wasn't quite right. Maybe it was the overgrown bushes that surrounded the house, or the branches of the trees that were slowly swaying above it. Unsettled or not, the two squirrels still walked slowly towards the light.

As they got closer, they began to see that the light was coming from an open doorway. They crept closer to the doorway, then, when they were only a couple of steps away, a voice spoke behind them which rooted them to the spot. "What are two young squirrels like yourselves doing out in the woodland at night?" The speaker was a great big fox. His tail was huge and bushy. His snout was long and twisted, and his eyes were large and his nails were as sharp as daggers. Dock and Nettle had never met a fox before.

They were both shocked and impressed with him, but they both thought, "Don't let him trick you". The squirrels had heard countless stories from Mrs. Thorn about foxes. Each story ended with an unfortunate creature placing its trust in a fox, which slyly tricked the unfortunate creature and gobbled it up. Dock and Nettle did not intend to be gobbled up, but they were already falling into the clever fox's plan without even realizing it. Dock and Nettle still hadn't answered the fox's question, so the fox answered for them.

"I expect you should be at home with your mother. She must be worried sick about you," said the fox, with a note of charm in his voice. The fox then pointed out at the dark woodland. "I saw you running out across my house. I called to you, but you didn't reply to me, so I went out looking for you. I thought that you must be lost," he explained.

Dock and Nettle didn't reply. Their mouths were hung open in shock. "Come inside," gestured the fox to the open doorway. "Take a break, and then I will help you find your way."

Dock and Nettle peered into the house. Through the open door, there was a lone table with a candle burning on it. It looked safe enough. The fox was close behind them now. "I'll roast some acorns for you before I take you home," he said softly.

The fox then nudged them in their backs, sending them tottering forward.

Dock had his eyes transfixed on the candlelight, but Nettle was blinking, his eyes darting around the inside walls of the house. The more his eyes flickered, the more terrified he became. On the walls, in plain sight, were hundreds upon hundreds of tails. He recognized them as the tails of different creatures he knew – mice, rabbits, hedgehogs and squirrels. Nettle instinctively bolted. He ran, not forwards but backwards. He shot through the fox's legs, out through the door and into the darkness of the woodland. When Nettle heard the door slam behind him, he turned his head as he ran, expecting to see Dock scurrying behind him, but Dock wasn't there. Nettle stopped. Dock was in the house, with the fox. The fox with the long, twisted snout and with an array of tails nailed across his walls.

Nettle stared at the house for some time, hoping that the door would swing open and Dock would come rushing out, but he didn't. The more time that passed, the more anxious Nettle became. Even though he was terrified, Nettle forced himself forward, one step at a time. As he inched closer to the house, he began to hear muffled sounds.

Nettle peered through the latticed windows. Dock was tied to a chair, next to the table with the candle. He was beginning to weep pathetically. "Oh, don't cry," said the fox. "I'll soon bring your brother back." The fox finished tightening the ropes and then dipped his paw into his pocket. He pulled out a handful of acorns, stuffed them into Dock's mouth and laughed. "Here, enjoy these."

Nettle ducked away from the latticed window as the fox then turned and strode towards the doorway. The fox flung the door open and with his great big ugly snout, sniffed at the air. "That squirrel is close," he muttered to himself. He drew a deep breath and called out in a very clear and charming voice. "Young squirrel. Follow my voice. Your brother is looking for you." Then, he catapulted into the darkness.

After jumping away from the window, Nettle had hidden himself behind the house and now slowly crept back to the doorway. He looked at the dark woodland and then to the doorway and then quickly scurried inside. When Dock saw him, he almost shouted in glee, but Nettle quickly raised his paw in warning. "He'll be back any moment," whispered Nettle. He bounded over to Dock and tried to untie the ropes. "The ropes are too tight," grunted Nettle.

"Then bite them," urged Dock.

Nettle opened his mouth and began chewing at the thick ropes.

"I know where you are," came a loud, booming voice. Nettle began chewing faster and faster until the ropes finally began to loosen.

"Don't worry, little squirrels, I have more acorns."

Dock managed to untangle the rest of the ropes and threw them down on the ground. As he did, the fox appeared in the doorway with a long grin planted on his ugly, twisted snout. The fox stepped in carefully and softly closed the door. As he did, his smile turned into a sneer, and the fox's charm turned to malice as he began to bare his teeth. The fox lunged at the two squirrels, but Dock and Nettle were both ready. They darted out of the way and quickly pushed the door open. Within moments, they were scrambling through the bushes of the woodland, their hearts pounding. They could hear the heavy breathing of the fox behind them, who was getting closer. "Quickly, Dock, up a tree," cried Nettle.

Dock didn't understand at first but then suddenly realized; not every creature can fly, and not every creature can climb trees. It was the only thing that Dock and Nettle could say that they were competent at. As they squinted in the darkness, they searched for the nearest tree and scrambled up it. The fox knew exactly which tree they were hiding in and tried his best to charm them down, but the squirrels refused to listen. They sat there, stuck their paws over their ears, and waited. They waited and waited until finally, the fox disappeared. Only then did they begin to speak to each other. "I think he's gone," said Nettle softly.

They both crept along the strongest looking branch and looked down, but all they could see was complete darkness.

"Now what," murmured Dock. "We can't stay here." Just then, the clouds above them began to part, allowing the moon to shine brightly. Bright rays of moonlight flooded the dark woodland, turning everything a strange translucent grey. The two squirrels smiled, because they thought the same exact thought at the same exact time.

"The snails," they both cried.

They began jumping from treetop to treetop in search of their slimy slow friends, and as they did, the fox suddenly reappeared below them, watching hungrily, trying to entice them back down to the forest floor.

"Come down," he cried. "I'll show you the way home."

The squirrels ignored the fox and continued searching for the snails. When they finally found them, they shouted out with glee. "They are here. They are still here. A long line of them."

The fox, who was still following them on the ground sneered at the snails and called up to the squirrels.

"Yes, yes, yes, I like snails too." The fox picked up one of the snails delicately in one paw, fixed his snout to its underside, and made a sickening sucking sound. "Delicious," he cried. "Come down and enjoy them with me."

Instead, the squirrels squinted down at the snails.

"We need to go this way," said Dock, pointing the opposite way the snails were crawling. Dock and Nettle immediately began bounding from branch to branch. Every now and then, the clouds would cover the moon, and the woodland would become encased in complete darkness. When this happened, Dock and Nettle calmly sat down and waited for the moon to reappear before they carried on. The disgusting fox followed them for a while, but then became tired of trying to coax them down, he reluctantly gave up and began slurping on the long line of snails. Dock and Nettle didn't hesitate and didn't look back, but they could hear that terrible slurping sound for a long time. The squirrels blocked the noise from their ears and carried on jumping until they finally entered the part of the woodland that they were familiar with.

Mrs. Thorn was just opening the door, it had barely opened a fraction when the two squirrels shot inside and almost knocked poor Mrs. Thorn down. They each held on to her and refused to let go until Mrs. Thorn began twisting their ears. "What is wrong with you two, and where on earth have you been?" she cried.

Dock and Nettle shivered and looked at each other. Neither of them felt brave enough to explain the whole story.

"W-w-we got lost," they both stammered.

Mrs. Thorn shook her head. "I bet you went following those snails, didn't you?" She waddled off to the kitchen and grabbed three bowlfuls of acorn soup. "No good ever comes from following snails," said Mrs. Thorn. Grandpa mouse had already eaten his acorn soup and was now snoozing in his chair.

Dock and Nettle looked at each other and breathed deeply. They were both amazed to be home and safe. Mrs. Thorn began slurping down her soup. The slurping sound made both Nettle and Dock jump up in alarm. They looked around them in fright, expecting the fox to jump out with a snail stuck to its snout. Mrs. Thorn shook her head again. "Whatever happened," said Mrs. Thorn, "please, do remember that you should always try to be back by supper time."

Dock and Nettle nodded their heads in agreement. That certainly was some excellent advice.

We all knew that bumping into the fox was going to be bad news, but we all also knew that Dock and Nettle were clever and brave enough to get themselves out of their sticky situation. The shocking thing we should all remember though is that they didn't happen upon the fox by accident. It was a disaster in their own making. If only they had shown more awareness at the very beginning, then they would never have had to go to such lengths to escape.

Late Autumn

Market Day

Look out for each other.

"I want you two on your best behaviour while we are at the market," instructed Mrs. Thorn to Dock and Nettle.

Dock and Nettle were extremely excited because Mrs. Thorn had agreed to take them both to the market. Mrs. Thorn usually went by herself and left Dock, Nettle and Grandpa mouse at home, but today, after much pestering from Dock, Mrs. Thorn had agreed to take them all to the market.

Dock and Nettle stood to attention with their tails straight, their chests puffed out and their heads eagerly nodding at every instruction and rule that Mrs. Thorn came out with.

"And don't wander too far away from me," said Mrs. Thorn finally, as they all headed through the door of the cottage and out into the breezy woodland.

"Mrs. Thorn, what will we get?" asked Dock nicely. They were just passing the crossroads where Mr. Magpie lived and were now turning down the path which lead to the market place.

Mrs. Thorn unraveled a long list she had written out. "A lot," she mumbled.

Dock took the list from her and read through it. Fifteen tins of earthworms, three sacks of acorns, one bag of caterpillars, two baskets of cherries and one can of slugs. "Where are we going to find all of this?" asked Dock.

Mrs. Thorn took the list back from Dock and smiled. "I know where to go," she said.

They trotted along the path until the trees finally began to thin out and a huge open clearing appeared. Dock and Nettle's eyes bulged. In front of them was row upon row of stalls, selling every type of food and item imaginable.

"Tail brushes, get your tail brushes," cried one vendor.

"Brand new, claw clippers. The best you'll ever use," cried another vendor.

"Right then, what do I need first?" mumbled Mrs. Thorn, taking out her list and examining it.

"Wow," cried Dock. "Look at all this stuff."

Nettle scuttled up to a stall that was selling an assortment of bugs, nuts and leaves.

Nettle then ran up beside Dock, grabbed a small wicker basket and began filling the bag with a paw-full of colourful grub.

"We should…" began Dock, who was now pulling on Nettle's tail, but was interrupted by the vendor of the stall, who suddenly jumped up from under the counter.

The vendor was a pheasant. A great big portly creature with a humongous tummy, a spindly neck and small beady eyes. When the pheasant jumped up, she knocked the table, and it would have spilled over if it wasn't for Dock's quick reactions.

"Anything else?" cried the pheasant shrilly.

Nettle turned, in search of Mrs. Thorn, but Grandpa mouse and her had both disappeared into the crowd.

"On second thoughts," said Nettle, apologetically.

He raised the wicker basket and was about to pour all of the grub back on to the large pile when the pheasant began to cough dramatically.

Her cough was meant as a subtle message to the two squirrels, but the cough quickly developed into a real cough and then a choke. After a few moments she was banging her wings on the table, causing the grubs and nuts to bounce up and down. When the pheasant finally gained her composure, she puffed her chest out and clucked.

"You can't put them back now."

Nettle looked at Dock, but Dock had no idea what they should do. Mrs. Thorn and Grandpa mouse had disappeared and the pheasant looked to be getting more and more agitated by the second.

The pheasant was now pointing at a sign that read.

"Exchange of feathers, grain and paint accepted."

"So, what do you have?" demanded the pheasant.

Dock and Nettle were both lost for words. They just stood there with their mouths hanging open.

"Hurry up," clucked the pheasant. "There are more customers waiting."

This was true, a long line of creatures were patiently waiting behind Dock and Nettle. They peered at Dock and Nettle suspiciously and urged them to hurry up.

Dock and Nettle were now very worried. They couldn't see Mrs. Thorn anywhere, and the pheasant was now starting to get angry.

"We're sorry," explained Dock. "My brother will go look for our mother to bring you the exchange."

However, the pheasant was not in the least bit convinced by this statement. She squinted at them and then clucked indignantly.

"I never saw your mother," she screeched. "You're lying."

"No, we aren't," cried Dock. "She's just over there, I know she is."

But the pheasant wasn't listening, she had worked herself into a tempest and was now clucking angrily.

"Hooligans, thieves, yobs, hoodlums, ruffians."

Each new word she clucked louder than the previous, until every creature nearby was staring at her stall and the two squirrels.

Creatures pressed in close to Dock and Nettle, who peered up at the tall, critical looking animals nervously.

"Hoodlums," agreed a tall, old badger. "They have that look about them."

"Where are your parents?" asked an elderly vole with a walking stick.

Dock and Nettle opened and closed their mouths, unsure of what to say. They were just about to try and explain themselves when a haughty looking rabbit with long pointed ears interrupted them.

"They don't have any parents," she blurted. "It's always the same story with these ruffians. No parents, no discipline."

There was a murmur of agreement from the other creatures who all now leaned in closer to Dock and Nettle.

"So what should we do with them?" declared the big badger slowly.

"Send them out of the woodland," clucked the pheasant. "They took my grub and now refuse to pay, it's what they deserve."

There was a roar of approval from the other animals, who had all formed a tighter ring around Dock and Nettle.

The two squirrels realized what was about to happen, tried to scamper through the crowd's legs, but were easily scooped up.

"Let go of us," cried Dock and Nettle.

They were being held up by their tails and dangled in mid-air, helplessly.

"It's too late for that now," cried the elderly vole.

"You should have thought about that before you damaged poor Mrs. Pheasant's stock," added the haughty rabbit.

"But we didn't do anything," cried Dock and Nettle.

This only upset Mrs. Pheasant more, who now began clucking hysterically again.

"Hoodlums," she screeched.

A bigger crowd had now gathered as the two squirrels were slowly carried to the edge of the marketplace.

Dock and Nettle kept squirming, but as hard as they tried to break free from the rough pawed claws of the creatures that were carrying them, there was simply no way they could escape.

"Let us go," helplessly cried Dock and Nettle.

"No," confirmed the big badger. "You are two naughty, parentless, hoodlums, and you deserve to be thrown out of this woodland."

The two squirrels had almost given up hope, when a loud, defiant call from outside the circle of creatures could be heard.

"Put them down." Mrs. Thorn was stood in front of the crowd with Grandpa mouse a few paces away, precariously balancing an assortment of shopping that Mrs. Thorn had stuffed into his arms. Mrs. Thorn stood there with a long spike in her paw. She pointed the spike at the big badger, and with a firmness that impressed Dock and Nettle, repeated her instruction. "Put them down, now."

"Who in woodlands name are you?" clucked the pheasant. Mrs. Thorn turned herself, so that all the creatures got a good look of who she was.

"I am their guardian," said Mrs. Thorn.

The vole with the walking stick hobbled out to the front, and waved her walking stick at Mrs. Thorn. "These two squirrels have just terrorized Mrs. Pheasant's stall. They are being evicted from…"

THWACK.

The long spike that Mrs. Thorn held in her paw whizzed through the air and struck the vole's thin walking stick perfectly. Mrs. Thorn reached over her back, tugged out another one of her own spikes and pointed it at the group. "Down," she repeated.

"Are we having a party?" asked Grandpa mouse, who was now rummaging through the bags of produce that Mrs. Thorn had handed him.

The group of creatures looked at the two dangling squirrels, then at the surprisingly dangerous looking hedgehog, and finally at the crazy old mouse. When Mrs. Thorn sent another spike flying through the air at the vole's walking stick, the creatures dumped Dock and Nettle on the ground and scattered off as if nothing had ever happened.

Dock and Nettle jumped up and bounded toward Mrs. Thorn, but Mrs. Thorn was not in a loving mood. "Home," she barked, relieving Grandpa mouse of the bags he was carrying.

They soon found themselves walking back down the woodland path towards their cottage. You could have cut the tension in the air with a knife, and no one dared utter a sound, except for Grandpa mouse, who was noisily humming to himself.

Eventually, Nettle gathered up enough courage to speak. "Who are our parents?" asked Nettle.

There was a long silence in which Mrs. Thorn searched for the right words with which to begin. "There are a lot of nice creatures in our woodland," she eventually said. "There are also a lot of dangerous creatures in our woodland. Some of them you have already met, and some of them you are yet to meet."

Dock and Nettle shivered when they remembered some of those creatures that they had already met.

"There are a lot of weird and silly creatures, like the ones you just encountered," sighed Mrs. Thorn. "How can they even think about throwing two small squirrels out of the woodland?" Mrs. Thorn looked like she was going to explode into a rage, but gradually calmed herself down. "There are also a lot of brave creatures," said Mrs. Thorn. Tears began to form in Mrs. Thorn's eyes. The tears began to well up before eventually trickling down her face. "Your parents were two of the bravest creatures I knew."

Dock and Nettle were huddled close to Mrs. Thorn and looked up at her while they walked. "Can you tell us about them?" asked Dock.

"Of course, my dears," sniffed Mrs. Thorn. "I'll tell you everything you want to know."

Mrs. Thorn was right, some grown-ups are weird and silly, but thanks to Mrs. Thorn, Dock and Nettle are now both safe and well. Hopefully, the experience will have taught Dock and Nettle to take responsibility of any needy creature that is younger or indeed older than them. The more we adopt the power of responsibility, the better a world we will all create.

Early Winter

Frozen Rescue

Luck can only do so much.

Dock and Nettle scampered outside as quickly as they could.

"Don't forget your scarves," wailed Mrs. Thorn.

The two squirrels darted back inside and grabbed their scarves. It was snowing, and not just a quick flutter. It had snowed non-stop all night, leaving a blanket of snow that reached the tops of their legs.

Mrs. Thorn had barely given them her permission to go outside, when the two squirrels bolted out of the front door and dived into the snow.

"Yippee," cried Dock.

He flung himself on his back and waved his arms, legs and tail into the snow, giggling as he did so. Nettle was already climbing up the large tree that hung over their home. He tiptoed along the biggest branch and began jumping up and down.

Just as Nettle was doing this, Grandpa mouse came trotting out of the house. Huge lumps of snow cannonballed down from the branch that Nettle was jumping on, and landed directly on top of Grandpa mouse, turning him into a snow-mouse.

"Grandpa," yelled Mrs. Thorn.

She scratched at the snow and pulled Grandpa mouse out.

"Did someone put the fire out?" he muttered, his teeth chattering together.

Mrs. Thorn scowled at the two squirrels, as she opened the door for Grandpa mouse. Before heading inside, she turned to them and said, "Don't get into mischief you two, and don't go near the stream," she cried.

The two squirrels had been up all night, talking about the games they would play in the snow. Mrs. Thorn had sat and listened to them with a smile on her face, but when they then started talking about playing by the stream, Mrs. Thorn jumped into the conversation and explicitly told them to stay away from the stream.

"The stream will be frozen," she explained. "Too dangerous. Do not go near the stream," she repeated sternly.

Once Grandpa mouse and Mrs. Thorn were safely inside, the two squirrels began to play. They threw snowballs at each other, and then they played hide and seek, using their snow-prints as a way to find each other.

"Found you," cried Nettle delightedly.

Dock was not happy about being found so quickly, but soon came up with another fun game to play.

"Let's make a snowball," cried Dock excitedly.

Nettle reached down, grabbed a handful of snow and lobbed it at Dock. The snowball exploded on his face in a flurry of white powder.

"Not that kind of snowball," spluttered Dock, wiping his face clean, and spitting snow out of his mouth.

"A huge snowball," cried Dock. "As tall as us."

Nettle liked that idea very much. He nodded his head and immediately leapt onto the floor, pushing and crunching large swathes of snow together. A short while later, the two of them were rolling an enormous snowball along. It came up to their waists, and then eventually came up to their heads.

"Where's my scarf?" cried Dock suddenly.

It seemed to have disappeared while they were making the enormous snowball, but no matter where they looked, they could not find it.

"Aha," cried Nettle. "There is only one place it could be."

"Where?" asked Dock, who was a little confused.

"In the snowball, of course," laughed Nettle. "It must have gotten caught up in the snow, while we were rolling it."

"Oh," sighed Dock.

He began to punch at the now massive snowball, but he just ended up hurting himself and then began jumping up and down in pain.

"Owowowow," cried Dock.

The snowball was so tightly packed together, that there was no way they could break it to pieces.

"I want my scarf back" huffed Dock.

Nettle kindly unwrapped the scarf from his own neck and gave it to Dock. As he did this, a brilliant idea popped into Nettle's head that caused him to jump up into the air.

"Let's roll it down from the top of the hill," he cried.

Dock and Nettle pushed the big snowball to the top of the nearby hill that overlooked the stream. Nettle was certainly more excited than Dock, who was becoming increasingly concerned about how big the snowball was becoming. Nettle didn't care one bit, he simply giggled at the idea of the massive snowball hurtling down a hill.

When they finally got it to the top of the hill, the snowball was almost twice their size.

"Now what?" squeaked Dock, panting to catch his breath.

"Now," began Nettle, "we watch it roll."

He gave it one strong push, which was enough to send it over the edge of the hill. The snowball rolled slowly at first, but pretty soon it was hurtling down the hillside. It bounced as it went, and then, at the moment it was at its fastest, it careered into a tree. The tightly packed snow suddenly exploded into a soft powdery mist, except for Dock's scarf, which appeared amongst the mass of white powder.

"My scarf," cried Dock.

The scarf was just about to settle in front of the tree the snowball had exploded on, when a gust of wind blew it past the tree and on to the ice of the stream. The stream that Mrs. Thorn had forbidden them to go near.

Nettle scurried down the hillside.

"No, Nettle, Mrs. Thorn told us not to," cried Dock.

Dock scurried down after Nettle. Nettle had already made his way past the tree and was gingerly tiptoeing on to the ice.

"Nettle," cried Dock.

"Don't be such a scaredy-squirrel," laughed Nettle. "It's not going to break."

But just as he said this, the ice began to split. Nettle stopped and looked down. The scarf was just in front of him. Nettle took one of his paws off the ice and leaned forward to grab it, but as he did this, the ice gave way, and he was plunged into the freezing cold water.

"Nettle," screamed Dock.

Dock began jumping up and down at the side of the stream in a panic. Nettle was usually a good swimmer, but with the stream being so cold it was preventing him from swimming properly. He began splashing amongst the broken ice, his head bobbing up and down.

"The," cried Nettle, before his head went under the water.

"The what?" cried, Dock.

Nettle's head bobbed back up.

"Scarf," he wailed, as he spat water out of his mouth.

Dock looked at the scarf that was laid out on the ice. He suddenly realized that he could use the scarf to help pull Dock out of the stream. But there was no way he could reach it without falling into the stream himself. Dock was readying himself to run back and get Mrs. Thorn when Nettle cried out again.

"Around your neck," he spluttered.

"Around my neck?" repeated Dock.

Dock touched his own neck and felt the soft woolen fabric of Nettle's scarf. Of course. Nettle had given him his scarf. Dock quickly yanked the scarf off, and, holding one end of the scarf, threw the other end to Nettle, who looked like he wouldn't last much longer in the ice-cold water. With his arms flailing about, Nettle managed to grab the scarf, and with a heave, Dock pulled him out of the stream.

When Dock and Nettle eventually made it back home, Mrs. Thorn went berserk. "I told you not to go near the stream," she yelled. "You could have drowned."

"Were they having swimming lessons?" croaked Grandpa mouse. "I used to be a swimming teacher," he muttered whimsically.

Mrs. Thorn set Nettle down next to the fire, wrapped him in a cocoon of blankets, and began making a pot of thick acorn soup. Mrs. Thorn was angry but relieved that the two of them were safe.

Dock explained the whole story to Mrs. Thorn, starting with the massive snowball and the missing scarf, and then how the wind blew the scarf onto the stream and how Dock nearly ran home to fetch Mrs. Thorn for help.

Mrs. Thorn listened intently, and in a kind, wise voice told them. "I can't stop you from doing what I think you shouldn't," she said. "There is one thing I want you both to remember though."

Nettle, who in between shivering and sneezing was trying to slurp up his acorn soup, spoke up. "What's that?"

Mrs. Thorn smiled and brought Dock close to Nettle. "Make sure you always look after each other."

It's lucky that Dock didn't go back to the cottage to get Mrs. Thorn. I don't think Nettle would have lived to tell the tale if that had happened. Luckier still was the fact that Dock had Nettle's scarf, an item which inevitably saved Nettle's life. But it wasn't all because of luck. These two squirrels share a bond that means they are always looking out for each other. Let's hope they keep that bond during their next adventure together.

Late Winter

Lost in the Dark

Within the darkest of dark, one can always find a light.

"Over there," cried Nettle to Dock.

The two squirrels had been busy picking holly berries ever since the sun rose, and their paws and faces were now stained red from the juice of the berries. Mrs. Thorn had instructed them to collect four baskets of ripe, tasty berries, but Dock and Nettle couldn't stop themselves from eating them. So far they had only filled one basket each. Nettle jumped onto a tall tree and scampered along the lowest branch which hung just above a huge clump of dark red berries.

"Are you sure?" cried Dock from the edge of the bush.

Nettle ignored his brother and reached down further. He stretched his paw down, but the berries were just out of reach, so, he curled his tail around the branch and stretched further still. Nettle just managed to grasp hold of the bunch of berries when the branch snapped and he fell straight into the bushes below. But not a sound was heard. Dock didn't hear a thump, nor did he hear Nettle cry out. All he heard was the crunching of leaves as Nettle passed through the bush, and then silence.

"Nettle, are you okay?" cried Dock. He listened for a reply, but didn't get one. Dock leapt onto the tree and scuttled along the same branch that Nettle had run along. He peered down at the area that Nettle had fallen into.

"Nettle," he yelled louder. Dock then sighed and looked around the woodland. "Looks like I have no choice," he muttered to himself. Dock took a step backward and then leapt into the bushes. Within moments, Dock cleared through the bush and was hurtling through darkness. Dock fell down a large, steep hole and began screaming as loud as his lungs would allow. He scrabbled at the sides of the hole but he couldn't grip the flaky wet soil. As he clawed at the sides, clumps of dirt and worms came tumbling down with him, and Dock began spinning like a leaf in a storm. After what felt like a lifetime, he suddenly crashed onto the floor. "Ouch," he cried. He looked up but couldn't see anything in the pitch-black darkness, and very quickly felt a whole plethora of emotions all at once. Loneliness, sadness, desperation and fear. He felt the emotions so suddenly and quickly that he could have easily just laid there and given up right there and then. But the sound of Nettle's voice cleared those suffocating emotions away in an instant.

"Dock is that you?" whimpered Nettle. Nettle was lying on the floor, just a few paces away from Dock. He turned to where he thought his brother was and reached forward to hug him. "Ouch," cried Nettle. "My leg, I think it's broken." Nettle whimpered as Dock sat down next to him and tried his best to calm him down.

Dock squinted his eyes, but couldn't see anything, then he felt around on the ground. "Oh, I found a berry," laughed Dock. "Do you want it Nettle?"

Nettle merely whimpered in reply, so Dock stuffed it into his mouth. "There must be a way out of here," muttered Dock to himself. Dock sniffed the air, searching for any clue that might lead them out, but all he could smell was the dampness of the hole and the berries that had scattered across the ground. It seemed hopeless, the only way out of the hole, that they knew of, was the same way they had arrived, but reaching that hole was impossible, and was made even more impossible with Nettle's broken leg. Then, just as Dock was about to search the ground for more berries, a light began to flicker directly in front of him, someone was holding a lamp and it was gradually coming closer to them. As the light drew nearer, both Dock and Nettle began to anticipate what kind of creature would be holding the light. At first, their thoughts hovered around the type of creatures they would least like to meet. A snake, a fox, a ferret, a stoat – but as the creature moved closer, Dock and Nettle were struck with the sense that this was a friendly creature. Maybe it was the way the lantern bobbed cheerfully from side to side, or perhaps it was the pitter patter that the creature's paws made as it came closer. When Dock and Nettle heard the creature hum a happy tune to itself, Dock and Nettle were pretty certain that they were going to be saved. Dock and Nettle assumed correctly that the creature was friendly, but they were not entirely correct that they were going to be saved.

The creature waddled right up toward Dock and Nettle. It had a long pink nose, small dotted eyes and ears, and huge pointed paws with extended mucky claws, one of which was grasping the lantern, while the other occasionally clawed at the ground. It was a mole.

As the mole stepped in front of them, Nettle opened his mouth to thank him for rescuing them, but before he could say anything the mole simply walked straight past the two squirrels as if they weren't there. The mole was evidently looking for worms. Every time he found one, he prodded it with his claw and then sucked it up noisily.

"Excuse me," said Dock, hesitantly. "We fell through into this hole."

The mole gave them a fleeting glance before scraping up more worms with its claws.

"Sorry," said Nettle. "Do you understand me?"

The mole sucked up another claw full of worms. "Yes, yes, you fell through a hole," it muttered.

Nettle nodded his head thinking that the mole would suggest how they could get out, but the mole merely looked down again and began walking on.

"Where's he going?" said Dock, a little frightened.

Nettle raised a paw and shouted out to the mole, who was now quickly walking away from them. "Could you help us get out?"

The mole carried on walking and muttered as he did so. "The tunnels are always changing."

Nettle just gawped as the mole carried on walking, with the two squirrels once again being shrouded in darkness.

"What are we going to do?" cried Dock helplessly.

Nettle tapped his paws together, trying his best to think, but just a few moments later another light appeared in the darkness. It was another mole. The mole bumbled along past them, the same way the first one had done, and replied to Dock and Nettle's pleas for help in exactly the same manner as the first one. What Dock and Nettle soon realized was that they were standing in the tunnels of the moles. All they knew about moles was what Mrs. Thorn had told them. She had said that they tend to keep to themselves and are only interested in worms. Dock also remembered Mrs. Thorn saying that they were incredibly vain. Dock remembered this just after the fourth mole wandered unhelpfully away from them. Nettle was beginning to get tired of begging for help, so remained silent as the next mole trundled past. "Your nails are looking particularly elegant today," said Dock, in the most charming voice he could muster.

The mole stopped in its tracks and turned towards the two squirrels. "Do you think so?" he cried. "I soak them in muddy water for the vitamins."

Dock could hardly see the moles claws but he nodded all the same. "And I love what you have done with your..."

Dock looked the mole up and down, trying desperately to find something that he could complement.

"Fur," jumped in Nettle. "We love what you have done with your fur. It really brings out the errr colour in errrr your..."

"Eyes," jumped in Dock. "It brings out the colour of your eyes."

The mole didn't react at first, he just seemed to let the words sink in, and then finally began stroking his fur coat.

"Thank you, thank you," cooed the mole. "It's nice when someone appreciates the effort you put into looking nice."

The mole suddenly spotted a worm wriggling down by his feet and quickly flicked it up in the air and slurped it down. Dock and Nettle tried very hard not to frown at this.

"Well you should definitely carry on doing whatever it is you are doing, you look great."

The mole nodded its head and looked ready to carry on, its eyes and nose kept flickering toward the floor, searching out for any wriggling worms.

"Handsome mole," started Nettle. The moles eyes immediately flickered back to them. "Before you go, could you be so kind as to tell us how to get out of this tunnel."

The mole held his lantern closer to them and then jumped back slightly in shock. "You aren't moles," he cried. "What on earth are you doing down here?"

Dock took a hopeful step closer to the mole and explained how they had been picking berries and had then fallen down a hole which had then brought them into this tunnel. "Well, enjoy yourselves," said the mole, as he began to trundle away. "The worms are really very delicious in this part of the tunnel."

"Wait," cried Nettle. "Could you help us find the way out?"

The mole ignored their request and just gave them a fleeting look and walked on. "It would be such a pleasure to walk out of here accompanied by the most handsome mole we have ever met," jumped in Dock, desperately.

The moles ears pricked up and he took a step backward before turning. "Come," he gestured, shaking his lantern from side to side.

Dock jumped up and pulled Nettle's arm around his shoulder, and they both scuttled forward after the mole. The mole seemed oblivious to the fact that Nettle had hurt his leg and couldn't walk properly. He quickly bumbled forward, chattering about all the things that he does to maintain his handsome complexion, while the two squirrels tripped forward in their effort to keep up with him. "Look at my teeth," said the mole.

He stopped, held the lantern to his face and opened his mouth to reveal a set of brown, chipped and misshapen teeth.

"Wonderful," lied Dock, gasping for breath.

"Yes, I clean them with stones you see, not just any old stones though, that would be lunacy, I use chalk."

Dock and Nettle tried to appear interested but in truth, they were simply struggling to keep up with the vain mole.

The mole led them through a complex network of tunnels. The mole turned right, left, then right again. The tunnels seemed never ending, and the moles vanity seemed never ending too. He talked about nearly every single part of his body and what he does to maintain his looks. The mole constantly talked about himself and didn't seem to recognize that he was talking to himself only. Dock and Nettle had dropped further and further behind the mole and were only just managing to catch sight of the turns he made.

"Come on," grunted Dock. "We need to keep up with him."

They watched as the mole, who was enthusiastically explaining about eyelash care, turned a corner. The bright light of the lantern quickly began to fade. The two squirrels were quickly losing their strength, but they pushed themselves forward with as much determination as they could muster. As they turned the corner, they collided with the mole. Dock, Nettle, the lantern and the mole all tumbled to the ground, but within a few moments the mole was up on his feet again, lantern in hand and walking off back the way they had come.

Dock and Nettle nearly hobbled to their feet and began scrambling back after the vain mole, fortunately, they didn't, because in front of them there was a speck of light. It wasn't from a lantern, it was a different kind of light, the distinct twinkle of daylight.

They both gave a sigh of relief and together, two brothers who could overcome anything, hobbled on forward into the twinkling winter sunlight.

Without hope, Dock and Nettle would never have found their way out. Without hope, Dock and Nettle would have quickly sunk into the darkness that enveloped them. No matter how dark the tunnel we find ourselves in, there is always a light at the end. Hope keeps the light burning and hope helps us find it.

Lightning Source UK Ltd.
Milton Keynes UK
UKHW030251080223
416610UK00011B/515